This book belongs to...

_____

www.TFMBooks.com

This book is dedicated
to my husband— my Petie Bird.
I love you, babe.

ISBN: 1500598704
ISBN 13: 9781500598709
Library of Congress Control Number: 2014915282
CreateSpace Independent Publishing Platform, North Charleston, SC

Petie Bird

Teaira Frazier Munoz
Illustrated by: Tea Seroya
Smiling Cheese Studio

He flew to the kitchen
to get a quick bite.
He had no idea
of what was in sight.

The family's dog, Percy,
then jumped up and roared.
The dog shoved the chair,
which screeched as it soared.

"Then Percy the dog was startled and roared.
He then shoved the chair, which screeched as it soared.
The chair pushed a button, which threw ice around.
Those ice cubes that flew let out a huge sound,
which woke you guys up,
so please…please…don't frown."

"Sometimes these things happen, so don't be upset.
Just take a deep breath; we'll clean up this mess.

"We know that what happened,
you didn't mean to do.
You're a part of this family,
and we really love you."

"Squaaawk, I love you guys too. I love you guys too."

CUSTOMER APPRECIATIONS...

THANK YOU for your valued business. I appreciate having you as a customer. I look forward to creating new and improved children's stories that may interest your child(ren). If you're interested in submitting a photo of your child(ren) **reading a TFM Book, wearing a TFM t-shirt, or holding a TFM mug** to be displayed on the customer appreciation page at **TFMBooks.com**, email i directly to: **T.FrazierMunoz@gmail.com**.
Please title the email, "Permission granted to display enclosed photo."

Warm Regards
T. Frazier Muno

m a native New Yorker who enjoys spending quality time with
family. I have always connected with the curiosity and optimism
children. This stemmed from my first job as a homework
inselor for Goodwill Industries. As a mother of two young,
veloping, impressionable boys, I often utilize children's literature
explore fundamental topics. The children's books that we share
en create great dialogue. Over the years, my love for children's
oks has matured, accompanied by life lessons that I have learned
m. Ultimately I decided to combine the two. This inspired my
cision to join the children's literature profession. My goal is to
ate contemporary, unique, quirky, and witty children's stories
th silver-lining lessons that families all around the world can
ate to. My children inspire me on a daily basis. It is my intention
continuously create new and improved children's stories.

Teaira Frazier Munoz

Mrs. Frazier Munoz also authored:
I Wonder How Terribly, is Speech Therapy?
My Brother & Me
and *Where's Luna the Lizard?*
Please feel free to visit **www.TFMBooks.com** for new releases,
upcoming book signings, and free activity sheets.